Mosey's Field

Written by Barbara Lockhart
Illustrated by Heather Crow

Schiffer Publishing Ltd

4880 Lower Valley Road • Atglen, PA 19310

For Alora and Damian, with happy memories of days at the farm. B.L.

To Roger, for his patience while Mosey's little paws
were not just in the art studio but all over the house. H.C.

When Mosey wasn't even a year old, he was already a long-legged, lumbering kind of dog. He loved chasing rabbits, herding chickens, barking at groundhogs, and sniffing just about anything.

He had a favorite place to nap, which was in the middle of a wide, flat field. He loved his field, and the big sky, and the way his house sat on the horizon.

On the first warm day in early spring, a disk harrow came through. It not only turned up the earth and a stone or two, but Mosey's napping place, too.

But that didn't stop Mosey. When the tractor left, he circled 'round and 'round and made another napping place, just as good as the first.

The next day, the planter came through. It made narrow trenches in the soil where it dropped corn kernels one by one. At the last minute, Mosey got up, but as soon as the planter left, he laid down again in his napping place, right on top of a few seeds.

And that was where he stayed. When he wasn't getting food from his dish by the back door, or chasing rabbits, or letting the family pet him, he laid in his napping place.

One morning, after a good rain, Mosey couldn't find his spot. He hung around the edge of the field and wondered where his napping place was. The field had become a sea of green.

In a few weeks, there were cornstalks shooting straight up like fence posts. Corn leaves burst out and grew so big they clacked in the breeze. When flies buzzed around his ears, Mosey ran between the rows and the leaves brushed off the flies. When he was hot, the leaves shaded him. After a rain, water dripped from the leaves and cooled him. Still, he wondered where his old napping place was.

Soon the stalks grew tall and the leaves crisscrossed each other, green upon green, so there were only tiny patches of sky. It was a field with secret places now, with long tunnels that beckoned him. One morning, Mosey decided to follow a corn tunnel to see where it led.

To his surprise, he came to town. It was still and quiet like it was in the middle of a nap. There was a post office and six houses with waves of heat rising from their roofs. There wasn't a single dog friend in sight. The only thing that moved was the mailman putting mail in one of the mailboxes.

Which made Mosey think of home. But all he saw was a wall of corn. Where was home?

At the other end of the cornfield, his family asked each other, "Where's Mosey?" And then they said, "Look, the corn's tasseled already!" just as you would say, "Look, the baby has a new tooth!"

Mosey spotted a rabbit. He had a special cry when he chased rabbits. "Errh, errh, errh," he squealed.

"That sounds like Mosey," one of his family said.

Mosey chased the rabbit but it ran into a corn tunnel and soon crossed through to another. Mosey couldn't cross the rows because the stalks were too close together. It was very frustrating.

Mosey kept running down the cornrow still hoping to see the rabbit. He came to a place that was missing some cornstalks. He could see a big patch of sky. This was it! This was his old napping place!

His family called and called. Mosey
paid no attention. He knew just where
he was. He stayed there a long time while
the rabbits teased him from a few rows
away. When he got hungry, he went
straight down the cornrow to his dish at
the back door.

It was a long, hot summer. Mosey hung out in the corn to keep cool, barked at the mailman, and snapped at flies. All the while, the corn grew higher and higher. By now, it was taller than anyone in Mosey's family. Slowly, it turned brown and dry. The leaves crackled and whispered in the wind. An ear of corn hung from every stalk. Nighttime came sooner than it used to.

One chilly morning, Mosey heard a monstrous noise. Something big and red with pointy teeth growled down the lane. It was heading toward his field! In another minute, it began to go right through the corn.

Mosey barked at it. He should warn his family about the monster! He ran and ran. The monster kept coming, its teeth aimed right at Mosey. Mosey ran all the way to his family's back door. There he stood, shaking. The monster came closer and closer. Mosey barked and barked.

"Look, here comes the combine with its corn picker," someone in Mosey's family said. "We'll be able to see all the way to town again." The combine swung its snout out to one side. Its teeth went between the rows to catch the cornstalks. It hummed and chugged and coughed while it cut the stalks, pulled off the ears, shucked the corn, and scraped off the kernels.

Corn flowed into the bed of the truck that waited close by while dry leaves and empty cobs fell to the ground. In a very little while, the whole field was harvested and the truck was piled high with golden corn.

Now the air was yellow with dust. The field was quiet with corn stubble. The tunnels were gone and so were the rabbits. Mosey was confused. He missed the leaves that filled up the sky. And where was his napping place?

While he was still safely at his back door thinking about things, the disc harrow came through and stirred up the earth. It turned under the corn stubble. Seagulls gathered behind the plow, looking for leftover corn and bugs. Then the field was brown again, and welcoming.

Slowly, Mosey lumbered out.
Before long, he found just the
right spot.

From there, he could see the whole sky, the edge of the field, and his house on the horizon. He turned 'round and 'round and settled down with a sigh, remembering the rabbits and the cool tunnels and the shining leaves crisscrossing green upon green.

Oh, it was wonderful to have his field back again, and everything right where he'd left it.

Corn

There are two major kinds of corn. In summer, we pull sweet corn from the stalks while the leaves are still green and the ears are full. The ears are covered with green leaves and yellow corn silk. When we shuck this corn (take off the leaves and the silk), we steam or boil the ears of corn, butter them, and eat the corn right from the cob. It is important to pick this corn when it is just right, not too young and not overripe.

The corn in this story is field corn and it is harvested in the early fall. It stays on the plant until the plant dries. The kernels are dry, too, and they are hard. Horses like to eat this corn as do pigs and other animals like deer. This corn can be ground into cracked meal for chickens. Field corn is also made into people food like breakfast cereal, cornbread, or corn oil. Because this corn can be stored in sacks or silos over the winter, it has been an important food for animals and people for thousands of years. People have even begun to use corn oil as a substitute fuel for cars.